Going to Playgroup

Catherine and Laurence Anholt

ORCHARD BOOKS

For Anna and Rebecca

ORCHARD BOOKS
96 Leonard Street, London EC2A 4XD
Hodder Headline Australia
Level 17/207 Kent Street, Australia, NSW 2000
First published in Great Britain in 1991
This edition published in 2005
ISBN 1 84362 853 8
Text © Laurence Anholt 1991
Illustrations © Catherine Anholt 1991
The right of Laurence Anholt to be identified as the author
and of Catherine Anholt to be identified as the illustrator
of this work has been asserted by them in accordance
with the Copyright, Designs and Patents Act, 1988.
A CIP catalogue record for this book is available from the British Library.
10 9 8 7 6 5 4 3 2 1
Printed in Singapore

Anna wasn't big enough to go to school.

And she wasn't
nearly big enough
to go to work.

But Mummy said she
was getting too big
to stay at home all day.

"It's time to make friends of your own,"
she said. "It's time to start at playgroup!"

"You'll need new shoes for playgroup,"
said Mummy.

"Who will help me put them on?"
said Anna.

"There will be a playleader, and lots of other children,"
said Mummy.

"Supposing nobody likes me?" said Anna.

She thought she'd take
her sister with her.

But babies don't
go to playgroup.

"Perhaps I'll just stay
at home," said Anna.

"Don't worry," said Mummy. "You'll love it when you get there."

"Look, here are all the mums and dads,
and that's Mrs Sams, the playleader."

"Hello," said Mrs Sams. "What lovely
shoes. Shall I help you put them on?"

"This is where we hang our coats

and this is Tom. It's his first day too."

Mrs Sams took Anna and Tom to meet
the other children. Some were having a
story, and some were...

sticking

cutting

drawing

building

painting

and rolling.

Everyone was busy.

"Will you make something nice for me?" Mummy asked Anna.

Then she went out of the door!

"Look, these teddies keep crying," said Tom.

"They're being very naughty."

"Shall we take them for a walk?"

Anna and Tom took their teddies to see

the rabbits

the guinea pig

the sand box

the water

the bikes

the slide

the home
corner

the bookshelf

the dressing-up
clothes.

Then the teddies stopped crying.

Mrs Sams needed two helpers.

All the children wanted to help.

But Mrs Sams chose Anna and Tom.
"You're both very helpful," she said.

Then all the children
queued for the toilets...

but some people
couldn't wait.

They all had to
wash their hands.

Tom forgot to
pull up his sleeves.

"Now walk back *quietly*," said Mrs Sams.

But some children ran.

"And try and sit still," said Mrs Sams.

But everyone jumped about.

Anna sat next to Tom.

The children sang some songs,

and clapped their hands,

and then they all ran outside to play.

"Hello," said Mummy. "Did you make
something nice?"

"Yes," said Anna. "I made a friend!"

"Will it be playgroup again tomorrow?"